Country I

Looking Back, Moving Forward

A Week With Hinie and Ellen

*In loving memory of
Henry and Ellen Van Gunst*

Dedicated to
their children,
grandchildren,
great-grandchildren,
great-great-grandchildren,
and all generations to come

Copyright © 2012 by Janet Hasselbring

ISBN-13: 978-0-9837685-6-2

All rights reserved. No part of this publication may be reproduced in whole or in part, stored in a retrieval system or transmitted, in any form or by any means, electronic, mechanical, photocopying, recording or otherwise, without the prior written permission of the publisher.

Snow in Sarasota Publishing
P.O. Box 1360
Osprey, FL 34229-1360
941-923-9201
www.snowinsarasota.com

Printed in the United States of America
by Serbin Printing, Inc. - Sarasota, FL
World Class Printing & Publishing
10 9 8 7 6 5 4 3 2 1

First Edition

Foreword

Country Dairy: Looking Back, Moving Forward—A Week with Hinie and Ellen, is a story about my parents, Henry and Ellen Van Gunst. It describes their life in the 1930s, when they started farming the land that is now Country Dairy. It was my privilege to grow up with my brothers and sisters in a loving home and to work alongside my dad on the farm for most of my life. I always dreamed of owning a dairy farm, and I am grateful to them for helping that dream become a reality. My parents saw farming change from using horses to using tractors; from using threshing machines to using modern, self-propelled combines. They were simple, hard-working folk, whose faith in God saw them through good times and bad. I watched them grow old together and have time to enjoy family, travel, and reading. One of their favorite authors was Vance Havner, a country preacher they knew, and with whom they could identify. I will always be proud to be their son.

Wendell Van Gunst, owner, Country Dairy

Author's Note

I, too, grew up on the farm that is now Country Dairy. As a child, I picked asparagus, cherries, and beans for my dad and helped my mom with her chores in the house and garden. So much has changed since then. I wrote *Country Dairy: Looking Back, Moving Forward—A Week with Hinie and Ellen,* because I wanted my children, grandchildren, and all visitors to the farm to appreciate its legacy and history.

From the farm store, look east past the main barn and the cows grazing in the pasture. Envision Henry guiding the plow as he walks back and forth across the field behind the workhorses, Maud and Daize. Now, look north up the hill past the grove of evergreen trees and imagine Ellen bending low in her garden, picking beans or hanging clothes out to dry on the clothesline. Finally, look across the highway to the west. Imagine Henry and Ellen watching the sun set from the front porch after their chores were done for the day (My dad claimed that on a clear day, he could see all the way to Lake Michigan). I hope this book helps you to appreciate the hard work, diligence and faith of my parents as they lived and worked on the land. Enjoy your visit!

Janet (Van Gunst) Hasselbring, author

This is a story of Hinie (Hī′ nee) and Ellen.
Together they lived on the land.
Hinie tended the farm and Ellen the house,
Living in harmony, hand in hand.

Come for a week to the house on the hill
Overlooking the countryside.
Watch as they toil from dawn to dusk
With God as their faithful guide.

On Monday, Ellen washes the clothes
And hangs them out to dry.
While they flutter and flap and
dry in the breeze,
She bakes an apple pie.

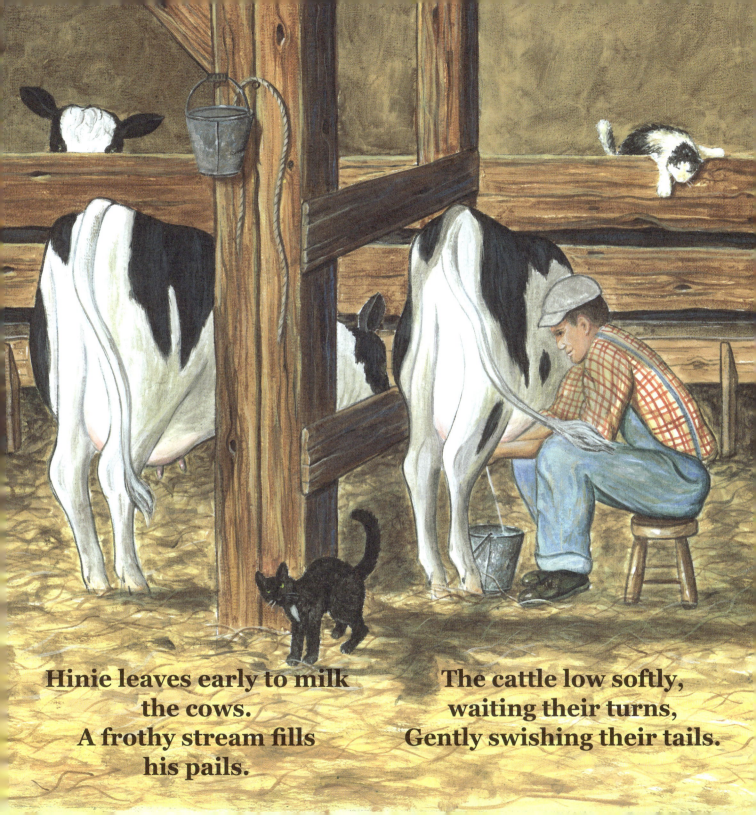

Hinie leaves early to milk the cows.
A frothy stream fills his pails.

The cattle low softly, waiting their turns,
Gently swishing their tails.

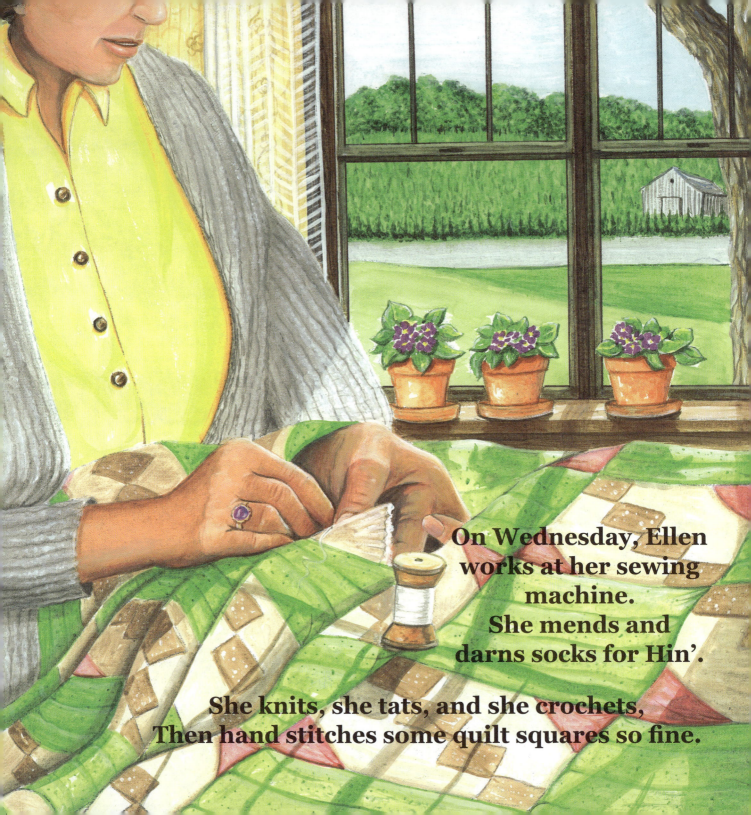

On Wednesday, Ellen works at her sewing machine.
She mends and darns socks for Hin'.

She knits, she tats, and she crochets,
Then hand stitches some quilt squares so fine.

Hinie's up with the sun to harvest the hay
With the hay rake it's rolled out to dry.
Then up the hayloader it travels along
Where it's piled on the wagon up high.

On Thursday, Ellen bakes her bread,
Mixing and kneading the dough.
She places the loaves into waiting tins,
Then into the oven they go.

Hinie works around the house.
He weeds the flowerbed.
He sprays the roses and trims the shrubs.
Then it's time for a slice of fresh bread.

Hinie loads the baskets
in the truck
And drives to the
asparagus field.

He snaps the tall, green, spindly stalks.
Then he's off to market with his yield.

In the evening
Hinie visits the chicken coop.
Chop! Off goes a plump hen's head!
He plucks its feathers and
soaks it well,
Before he and Ellen go to bed.

On the Sabbath, Hin' and Ellen go to church, Dressed in their Sunday best.

Then home for chicken with all the trimmings, And an afternoon of rest.

Seven children graced their home—
Four daughters and three sons.
More clothes to wash, more socks to darn,
More mouths to feed—cinnamon buns!

Many years passed—
Hinie and Ellen were tired.
It was time to pass on the torch.

They sold the farm to Wendell, their son,
And went out to sit on the porch.

Birds are singing, crickets are chirping,
With nature in perfect accord.

A breeze is blowing,
the sun is setting,
Perfect peace—with each
other and their Lord.

Hinie and Ellen have gone to heaven.
They've watched their last sun set.
But surely as the sun will rise each day,
Their lives we will never forget.

The farm has changed since they lived here.
Country Dairy is now its name.
But the lessons learned from
Hinie and Ellen—
Hard work, diligence, and faith—
are the same.

The End

Moo School Facts

DID YOU KNOW?

1. Country Dairy owns approximately 2,400 cows and milks about 1,400 of them at a time.

2. The average cow at Country Dairy produces 9 gallons of milk a day. The butterfat in that milk would make 15 ice cream cones.

3. The top cow at Country Dairy, during her best season, produces 23 gallons of milk (37 ice cream cones) a day.

4. Country Dairy produces enough milk in a week to fill three large swimming pools.

5. A cow gets milked three times a day. Each milking takes about 10 minutes, so cows only work 30 minutes (½ hour) each day.

6. Cows get lots of sleep and can eat as much as they want. Well-fed and comfortable cows produce the most milk.

7. Cows eat soybean meal, ground corn, corn, alfalfa, and hay silage. The average cow eats 100 lbs of food in a day. That would be the equivalent of a human eating 400 hamburgers!

8. A cow lives to be about 12 or 13 years old.
9. Cows have 5 stomachs to digest all the roughage they eat.
10. When cows "chew their cuds" they are "rechewing" their food and passing it along from one stomach to another.

Did you know that all these products come from milk?

Cheese
Ice-cream
Butter
Eggnog
Cottage cheese
Cream cheese
Sour cream
Chocolate milk
Whipping cream
Buttermilk
Yogurt

About Country Dairy

Country Dairy is a three-generation centennial farm, located one and a half miles north of New Era, Michigan. Andrew Van Gunst purchased the land when he was 21 years of age. He was just a boy when he and his family came to this country from the Netherlands. A year later his family members died of tuberculosis. As an orphan, he worked on farms for his room and board. In 1901, he purchased 40 acres of his own. In 1957, he sold the farm, now 80 acres, to his son, Henry. Henry's son, Wendell, purchased the farm in 1968 and transformed it into a dairy operation named Country Dairy. Tours of the dairy farm and its operation are offered year around, and a farm store serves meals and ice cream and sells a variety of products. Country Dairy's products are bovine growth hormone (BGH) free.

For more information visit
www.countrydairy.com

About the Author

Janet (Van Gunst) Hasselbring is a retired educator and musician from the West Michigan area. She resides in Spring Lake, Michigan, near Hoffmaster State Park with her husband, Don, and her yellow lab, Maximus. They spend their winters at Pelican Cove in Sarasota, Florida.

Janet is the 2010 Hertel First Place Winner of the Children's Story category from the Maranatha Christian Writers' Conference.

About the Illustrator

Bruce DeVries is a self-taught artist who works from his home studio in West Michigan. One of his most recent accomplishments was illustrating the book "The Big Day Is Here!" Bruce lives in Fruitport, Michigan, and when he isn't illustrating children's books, you can find him outside as he also is an avid gardener.

Also by Janet Hasselbring

Tales from Pelican Cove

Come along on a journey to Pelican Cove and learn about the different birds and plant life that inhabit this wonderful place. Each book in the Tales From Pelican Cove series has an educational section making it not only entertaining, but a learning tool.

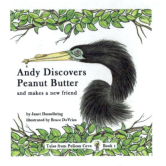

Andy Discovers Peanut Butter – *Book 1*

Pelican Cove is alive with wildlife everywhere, swimming, diving and flying. Bubba, however, has been traveling inland, away from the cove, for some time now and Andy is bound and determined to find out why. When he confronts his friend, Bubba reveals his secret and decides to make Andy his partner.

Andy Discovers Peanut Butter focuses on the do's and don'ts of feeding wild animals human food and other related issues. For more information on this subject go to the Save Our Seabirds, Inc. website: **www.saveourseabirds.org**

What Do You See, Mrs. Night Heron? – *Book 2*

In this delightful poem, Mrs. Night Heron is sitting on her nest overlooking Pelican Cove. As she awaits the birth of her chick, she is entertained by the wildlife of the cove. Learn about Florida's spectacular wild birds and the interesting nests they build. Go on an Egg Hunt! If you look closely, you will find Mrs. Heron's egg hidden in each illustration!

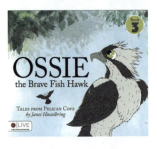

Ossie The Brave Fish Hawk – *Book 3*

At Pelican Cove, it's summer and the fish are jumping. Ossie, the osprey goes fishing but every time he catches a fish, Baldwin, the bald eagle, steals it. How is Ossie going to be able to feed his family with Baldwin, the pirate, on the loose? Must he really leave his beloved cove to build a new nest elsewhere? Come along on a journey to Pelican Cove and learn how Ossie helps Baldwin fight off another pirate and ends up gaining a new friend and saving his nest at the cove.

Janet's books are endorsed by Save Our Seabirds, Inc., a totally nonprofit organization dedicated to rescuing injured native and migratory birds promptly, treating their injuries and releasing rehabilitated birds back into the environment.

www.saveourseabirds.org